DREAMWORKS

HOME

Tip's Tips on Friendship

adapted by Sheila Sweeny Higginson

illustrated by Thies Schwarz

Ready-to-Read

Simon Spotlight
New York   London   Toronto   Sydney   New Delhi

SIMON SPOTLIGHT

An imprint of Simon & Schuster Children's Publishing Division

1230 Avenue of the Americas, New York, New York 10020

First Simon Spotlight paperback edition February 2015

For information about special discounts for bulk purchases, please contact Simon & Schuster Special Sales
at 1-866-506-1949 or business@simonandschuster.com.

Manufactured in the United States of America 0316 LAK

10 9 8 7

ISBN 978-1-4814-2611-4 (hc)

ISBN 978-1-4814-2610-7 (pbk)

ISBN 978-1-4814-2612-1 (eBook)

I am Gratuity Tucci.
All my friends call me Tip.
My world changed when the Boov
took over the planet.

There were aliens everywhere.

One night I met a Boov alien.

He was not like the other Boov.

First of all, his name was Oh.

(Strange, I know!)

He actually talked to me.

He did not try to send me away.

Oh and I did not get off to
a good start.
I was mad at all of the Boov
for stealing Planet Earth.
Oh thought humans liked
that the Boov had arrived.

Here is my friendship tip number one: Do not get mad and say something you will be sorry for later.
Call a truce instead!

Oh said he was
a technology superstar.
He fixed my broken car
so I could find my mom.
Tip number two: Friends help
fix one another's problems.

I was trying to hide from the Boov.
I did not want to give one
a ride in my car!
But Oh had fixed my car.
Plus, he said he knew where
to find my mom.
Tip number three: Friends
always repay a favor.

Oh liked to tell jokes.
So I taught him my favorite one.
"Knock-knock," I said.
"Who is there?" he replied
"Interrupting cow," I answered.
"Interrupting—"
"MOOOOO!" I mooed.

I did not let him finish.
Oh loved it! He mooed for ten
minutes straight!
Tip number four: Friends laugh
at one another's jokes—
even the bad ones.

Oh said we needed to go to Paris
to find out where the Boov
had moved the humans.

As we flew to Paris,
I turned on some music.
Soon we were both dancing.
It was a Boov groove!
Tip number five: When the going
gets tough, tough friends dance!

Dancing made Oh feel hot,
so he jumped into the ocean
to cool down.
He was gone for hours and hours.
I thought I had lost him forever.

Oh came back with plastic rings
to snack on.
(Boov like to eat strange things.)
He offered some to me.
Tip number six: Always offer
to share with your friends!

I felt mad and sad that Oh had
disappeared for such a long time.
I had to tell him why
I was so upset.

Boov do not understand what
it is like to be sad and mad.
I tried to help Oh understand.
Tip number seven: Friends tell
one another how they feel.

The next day, Oh and I arrived
in Paris.
The Boov had made a lot of changes.

The leader of the Boov,
Captain Smek, was trying to
find Oh, but Oh did not want
to be found.
We were there on a mission to
find my mom.

So we had to sneak Oh around Paris.
I had an idea.
Oh loved his new look!
Tip number eight: Help your friend
when he or she needs you.

Oh found out where my mom was
from a secret Boov computer in Paris.
The Boov had relocated her
to Australia.
I was so happy!
I thanked Oh many times.
Tip number nine: Friends always
remember to say thank you.